Nine Lives:
A Reunion in Paris

Marty Gervais

Cities
of the
Straits
Series

Cities of the Straits Chapbooks
Three Fires Confederacy
Waawiiyaatanong
Windsor, ON ✦ Detroit, MI

Copyright 2020 by Marty Gervais

All Rights Reserved No part of this book may be used or reproduced in any manner without written permission except in the case of brief quotations embodied in critical articles and reviews. Please direct all inquiries to the publisher.

First Edition. June 2020

Library and Archives Canada Cataloguing in Publication

Title: Nine Lives : a reunion in Paris / Marty Gervais.
        Gervais, C. H. (Charles Henry), 1946- author.
Description: Series statement: Cities of the Straits | Short stories.

Identifiers: Canadiana 20200217739
        ISBN 9781988214412 (softcover)

Classification: LCC PS8563.E7 N56 2020 | DDC C811/.54—dc23

Cover Image: Marty Gervais
Cover Desgin: D.A. Lockhart
Book Layout: D.A. Lockhart

Published in the United States of America and Canada by

Urban Farmhouse Press
www.urbanfarmhousepress.ca

The Cities of the Straits Chapbook series honors both Windsor, Ontario, Canada and Detroit, Michigan in namesake. Chapbooks in this series highlight the best non-fiction, fiction, and poetry submitted to us. It is published annually.

Contents:

Preface	/1
Dear Sarah	/5
Dear Jacklyn	/7
Dear Samantha	/9
Dear Victoria	/11
Dear Emily B	/13
Dear Emily A	/15
Dear Paige	/18
Dear Jessica	/20
Dear Krysten	/24
About the Author	/31

Preface

This is a fictional story. I really only have one daughter. But when I was in France a few years ago, accompanied by these nine lovely young women — students from the University of Windsor — we were down by the Seine drinking red wine one night and some young men — very drunk — strolled by, and asked why I, an old man, was in the company of all these beautiful women. Before I could reply, one of the students, Krysten, piped up, "This is our Papa!" (She spoke French) They stepped back, surprised, and pointing at the women made a count. They stammered, "You were married nine times?" Again, before I could reply, Krysten explained, "He was married to each of our mothers, and this is our reunion where we get to meet each of our half-sisters. Nine different wives, nine different mothers."

The young man, a little shocked, then edged forward and started looking at each of the women, and then turned back to me, and suddenly exclaimed, "I can see it in the eyes…Definitely sisters! Definitely your eyes!" He moved back again, and shook his head in disbelief, and stuttered, this time saying, "That … is a good life!"

And so much later, on the flight back to Canada, I started writing this piece.

I must thank was Doug Glover and **Numero Cinq on-line magazine** for first publishing this.

That last night in Paris, we went down to the river with two bottles of Burgundy wine. We watched the river come alive with lights. The young boys cavorting in the darkening landscape. We waved away the men hawking cigarettes and small bottles of wine. Saw a man coaxing a thin young woman to join his five buddies. The two argued under the lamplight along the wall facing the Seine. Her gestures clearly conveying her displeasure. Finally, she seized her friend by the forearm and pleaded with him to come away. And when he resisted, she turned and marched back up the ramp to the street above. I sat silently watching and sipping red wine out of a plastic cup, half listening to the nine of you trading stories of one another, talking about your mothers, my nine wives. You, my nine daughters. Nine different mothers. Nine halfsisters meeting for the first time. A rendezvous in Paris. These are your stories.

Dear Sarah

You danced along the Seine in the fading light above the rooftops, the river rejoicing in the thin shadows that lift and play on a cobblestone night. You are the first, your mother a gypsy I met in Bologna, a young girl riding the commuter train. I'd see her every morning on my way to the library. Her hips sashaying through the aisles, dark and brooding eyes, and a smile that lit up the faces of men everywhere. I spoke to her one dark morning when it was raining, and I let her take my umbrella and trailed after her to a small albergo in the fish market. A room overlooking the street. I watched her unlatch the big windows that ran from floor to ceiling, and she opened them to the rain, the men in the market hurrying to cover the tables with tarps, and scrambling for shelter. She made me tea, boiling up water on a small stove down the hallway, and I sat on the edge of the bed, and cupped a rounded clay mug, and I listened to her to speak about her family from Vienna. Street musicians. How her father wasn't happy with her — she couldn't play the fiddle to save her soul. But she could dance. They would play, and she would dance. Her body, light and lively, her skirts catching the wind... That afternoon, she danced in the dark room above the fish market, moving with such grace, such wonder. We stayed for a week, and I quit my job to join her family in Vienna where we were married... It couldn't last. I knew that. Perhaps even that day in Bologna. I knew nothing of her pregnancy until I received a telegram telling me of your birth. By then I had crossed the ocean, returned home and was working at the University of Toronto medical library. I disappeared into the labyrinth of stacks, and sat in its silence and read about you: *She is a daughter. Dark eyes, delicate hands. Looks nothing like you.*

Dear Jacklyn

I met your mother in Krakow. I had gone to the opera house in the late afternoon. Shocked to hear the trains rumbling so close by, just outside the tall narrow windows, the place shuddering like a startled puppy. It annoyed me and took my attention away, and when I looked up I saw her across the aisle. She was by herself. Her hand clutching a leather purse or bag. A scarf covering her head. She glanced at me, and gave me that look as if she knew me, had met me somewhere. I instantly turned away. I didn't want her to think I was staring, but I wondered what it was about me that caught her attention. Out of the corner of my eye, I could see that she had turned to look at me again. I tried to fix my attention on the concert program. The pianist was playing *Polonaise in A-flat major*. I was in Krakow on a research grant. I was searching for a family that I had been swept up by the Nazis in the war — it was thought they were Jews, and both the mother and father had been arrested and sent to the camps. They perished there. My interest, however, was a boy who had survived, and had lived with an uncle who worked as a shoemaker. I was having trouble finding people who knew him. That afternoon when I walked out into the courtyard outside the theatre, your mother was there. Once again, she glanced at me, but this time, I nodded and smiled. She paused, then shyly stepped over in my direction, and we stumbled through introductions. I knew no Polish, but she knew some English ... Three months later, we were married. I was the only English-speaking person at the wedding. My parents refused to be there. They still weren't happy with my marriage. We lived in a small flat above a café. I continued my research and hoped to return to Toronto, but we ran into difficulties with her emigration to Canada. I had to leave, but I promised to smooth the way for her to join me. I was very much in love. At night, in the four-room flat in Krakow, I would sit with her in the kitchen. A bare tungsten lightbulb dangling above us, cupboard doors sagging on their hinges, the floor cold against the soles of our bare feet. I held her hands in mine, and we talked about the future. A life in Toronto. That April when I left, I promised I would return by summer. She need not take anything. But after a few months of wrangling with immigration authorities, and getting nowhere, sadly I gave up. It was in September that she told me she was expecting. It took your mother another 10 months before she let me know I had yet another daughter. After a year, she sent me a photograph. My second born.

Dear Samantha

I left a steamer trunk behind in Bologna with my first wife. Some day I might let you see it. I have it stored away — its contents a miscellany of notebooks, post cards, dried flowers, Russian watches and hats, things I picked up on my trips to the book fairs in that city. I met your mother one night in January when I decided to check out *Tre Poetes*, a café of the three poets. The waiter was leaning up against the doorframe, a cigarette dangling from his lips as he spoke, the ceiling fans whirling like lazy dancers. Your mother was clearing the tables. The most beautiful smile as she gazed up. I am not sure why I did what I did — it was not at all characteristic of me to be so bold, but I reached out and took her wrist and thanked her. Surprisingly, she smiled. She never spoke a word. Months went by before I saw her again. This time at the market. Three days before I was returning to Toronto. She recognized me and nodded. I can't believe what happened next. I cancelled my flight. The next afternoon, we were in the plaza when it started to rain, and we ran for cover under the colonnaded streets, and found shelter in a noisy cramped café. A soccer game blinking away on the TV behind the bar. Italy versus England. We could hardly hear each other, but there was something special in that moment. We slept that night on the third floor of the same albergo that I had shared with my gypsy wife. A different room. I told her all about the

Sarah. Men do that. They talk. Maybe it's to make sense. Maybe it's to boast. Maybe they think women are interested. We talk. We talk too much. But that night, she didn't care as we snuggled in this quilted winter night. We were married in the summer. Our wedding night in the big room at the front of the house.

I am not sure why your mother left me. I returned home to find her suitcases packed, and a man I had never seen conveying them to the car outside. We were still residing in Bologna. I knew of your birth from a newspaper clipping that arrived in the mail nine months later. *An eight-pound baby girl.*

Dear Victoria

I was at the post office in Rome when I met your mother. She was arguing with the clerk over a package that had arrived at her home in Malta. Somehow it had been ripped open, and its contents damaged. She wanted compensation, maybe an apology — I am not sure. It made little sense. She just wanted someone to talk to. She was getting nowhere, when suddenly she began directing everything at me. I nodded. I frowned. I sighed. Finally I was holding her hands as they dipped up and down, her dark eyes fixed upon me as if I could solve all the problems in the world. I am good listener sometimes. Maybe it's because I really have little to offer. Maybe it's because I really don't care. I'm not sure. Maybe I care more than I think. In any case, for her, I was the only one willing to hear her story. Soon we had wandered far from the post office, and we were walking in the square— the afternoon light fading over tiled rooftops and the city exhaling its tired sounds. Your mother was the sweetest woman I had ever met. I was leaving that night for Sicily and asked her if she wanted to join me. I drove a white 1964 Fiat 500. Its brown leather seats slightly ripped. Our suitcases taking up the entire back seat. We drove through the night, and she talked about her family in Malta, and begged me to join her. She wanted me to meet her parents. They owned a small hotel, and sometimes she worked in the kitchen. I couldn't resist.

12

A month later, we sailed for Malta. Two months later, we were married. Our honeymoon in a village by the sea. Four days. We never left our room. A year passed and I was there for your birth. The doctor bundled you up and carried you down the narrow hallway, his shoes clicking on the tiled floors. *Your beautiful beautiful girl.* Your mother left me in six months. I sailed to the mainland. I made my way to Prague. Another research grant. This gave me time to think.

Dear Emily B

I wasn't surprised to meet you and see a camera in your hands. You are so much the image of your mother. I can't forget that moment when I met her in Prague. She was that lean, and elegant woman who moved right in front of me just as I stepped out of a taxi. She apologized for standing in my way. I noticed she was holding a Leica. She was photographing the St. Vitus Cathedral that towered above the city. It surprised me that she spoke English. I paid the driver and turned to her again, for it seemed she was waiting for me to say something. Instead, she apologized awkwardly, then offered to carry my leather bag, or at least my satchel. I smiled and told her I really didn't mind — she had not inconvenienced me in any way. *Well, can I buy you a coffee?* I agreed. We made our way to a small café. We were the only ones there except for the owner who was sweeping the floor. Your mother was a photographer then for a small news service. I know she gave this up a long, long time ago. That day her assignment was to photograph the restoration work being done on the cathedral. I asked her if she was married, and this surprised her. Actually she seemed offended. It wasn't the kind of thing you should ask anyone. But she did tell me she had just broken up with a man that she loved very very much. He was notary, and made good money, and was well respected in the city. She had intended to marry him, but one morning she spotted him at the train station embracing a tall beautiful woman who was boarding the train. When she asked about this woman, he denied it. She was crushed. She stopped seeing him three months ago. That night, when I was unpacking some of the research material I had brought with me to the city, there was a soft knock at the door. It was your mother. She asked if I might join her for a drink. The rest is history. We were married in Prague. A small wedding. That night we drove to the Baltic coast. We stayed two weeks. It rained five days straight. We never left our rooms. Our meals were delivered from a nearby café. We were married for 17 months. You were born at Christmas when I was back in Toronto, struggling with a book I was researching. I received a phone call that night. A snowy night from your grandfather. He seemed emotional. His first words were: *She's a girl. A little girl. That's good.* The marriage was doomed from the beginning. She wanted a career. I didn't care, I guess. Or that's what she claimed. It was always about what I wanted, never about her. I complained too much. I left for France that summer. You were eight months old. Your mother packed my suitcase and told me to leave. When I got to Paris, and walked from Gare Bercy to a nearby hotel, and opened my suitcase, there was a tiny photograph of you in the garden of our house in Prague. You were sitting on a blanket. Freckles, and pushing back strands of hair. I wrote you a letter and hoped your mother might read it to you one day. You were my fifth daughter. I told your mother nothing of the others.

Dear Emily A

I was surprised to find out that you played basketball. Your mother was an opera singer, as you well know. She gave it up by the time you were 12, and she had the most beautiful voice. In the early mornings when we were first together, I would be wakened by her at the other end of the flat we rented in High Park in Toronto. As I say, I was surprised when we first spoke. I could see myself driving to the games in high school gymnasiums. I know nothing of the sport. But I look at you and beneath that athletic build is someone with culture, with intellect, someone who quotes philosophy and poetry as easy as breathing … You are like your mother that way. I met your mother when I was tired of Europe. I returned to Toronto, and within four or five months, I was looking for a job out west. I met your mother in Banff. I was at a conference. She was a singer, and had just finished a run in Calgary, and had joined some girlfriends for a weekend away. I was at the Rankin Hotel on the main drag. She was staying there too. We met in the lobby. I was reading the paper. She saw the headlines about the federal election taking place Monday, and asked if I was going to vote. *Yes* I said. *Of course and what about you?* She waved her hand as if to dismiss the whole affair. *Well sure*, she said. *But really what's the point? The same old stodgy bastards will get elected, right?* I nodded, and then laughed. She smiled coyly.

I asked lamely, *What brings you to Banff?* From there, we traded stories. I'm not sure what impressed your mother about me. But she was eager to hear all about my stories from Europe. She had always dreamed of singing opera in Bologna or Milan. I spoke about the colonnaded streets of the north, or the old opera house in Bologna. And the place by the sea in Malta. About traveling by train to the Baltic and Paris and Frankfurt. That afternoon, we walked down to the Bow River. I rented a canoe and we kept close along the bank of the river. I told her its landscape reminded me of the poetry by Gary Snyder. I tried my best to quote from his work, and told her he was friends with Kerouac, that Kerouac had actually written a book about him called *The Dharma Bums*. The next day I returned to Toronto and for the next three months, I worked on my book. That fall, I flew to Paris for another conference. I hadn't followed up with your mother at all since Banff. I had promised to write, and of course, I did not. She didn't either. But there I was making my way along Git-Le-Coeur one night when I ran into her. We stood in the street, police sirens wailing in the distance, and the street lights twinkling all around us, and it was as if we were two long lost children finally finding one another. I remembered telling her in Banff all about Snyder and Kerouac, and told her she ought to check out Hotel de Vieux Paris, the place where Ginsberg and Burroughs had stayed. That night, I walked her back to her hotel. She was in Paris to attend an opera. A friend had landed a job with a company traveling through Europe. She got me tickets, and we sat together the next night. I was in the city for a week. She spent two nights with me in a hotel with a view that overlooked the topsy-turvy coloured rooftops of Paris. I could see both *Le Palais de Justice* in the distance, and the *Pont Neuf*. By the fall we were married. We moved to a High Park in Toronto. That winter we went down to Grenadier Pond, and with the softly falling snow all around us, we promised one another we would stay together for ever. Forever turned out to be five months. I really did love her. But we argued over everything. Religion, politics, poetry, whether black was really black, nutella over chocolate, Mac versus PC, and the Leafs over the Canadiens … I finally moved out. You were born eight months later at the hospital right at the end of Roncesvalles. A simple snide handwritten note: *Your daughter was born yesterday. How many does that make now?*

Dear Paige

I saw a Polaroid shot of you when you were four. You wore glasses. Your smile was tender and earnest. You wore knee-high stockings, patent leather shoes and ribbons in your hair. I was dumbfounded and baffled as to why I was receiving this picture. That's when I learned of your birth. That's when I learned that you were the seventh daughter. I don't blame your mother for keeping it from me. We were married for four months when she got pregnant. I knew nothing about it of course otherwise I might have stayed. But she kept it from me, perhaps to get back at me for leaving her. We were living in Saskatoon. I was working at the library. She was doing graduate work in English Literature at the university.

But it was in Windsor, Ontario where we met. I was back in that region for some consulting assignments with the city over setting up its archives. I had become a specialist on French settlements. She was working part-time at the museum there. We went out a few times. I didn't think she was too serious, but when I got this appointment in Saskatoon, she asked me if I might consider living together. That's when I popped the question. We were married in a civil service at City Hall. Our honeymoon was a bit old fashion. We drove to Niagara Falls, and rented a motel room. From there, we drove to Saskatoon. I have to tell you, we really enjoyed each other's company. And liked the same movies, same foods.

And like me, she gravitated to the scholarly and was serious and sober-minded in the way she looked at the world. She was maybe a little shy, or so it seemed, but truly she was a confident woman, and her smile won me over every time. I don't think I ever loved your mother. It was more a matter-of- fact kind of marriage. Convenient. The day I left, I called a taxi and moved into a rooming house in town. I quit my job two months later, and moved back to Windsor.

Dear Jessica

Your mother had red hair. I spotted her late one afternoon in Dublin. I had never been to Ireland before. This was the first time. A holiday finally. I was still smarting over the other marriages. Feeling pretty low. Wondering what had gone wrong. And daughters scattered across the globe. The taxi driver was welcoming me to the city, but I wasn't really paying attention. We sped past a blur of shops, doorways, and men congregating outside of pubs. That's when I heard the driver tell me it was Bloomsday, the anniversary of when James Joyce and Nora Barnacle went out walking together for the first time, the day on which the novel *Ulysses* takes place. The 16th of June, 1904. A humid day in Dublin. *You heard of Mr. Joyce?* he asked. I nodded. *Of course*. And smiled. The driver's face fragmented in the rear view mirror. He was smiling broadly and still talking. I got out at Finn's Hotel. I knew that's where Nora had worked as a chambermaid. I stepped out into the street, telling the driver I wanted to walk. Of course, I made my way to Merrion Square. After all that's where James and Nora met, and passed by 68 Clare Street where Samuel Beckett's father ran his business and where Beckett would write *Murphy*. Soon I was immersed in the culture and literature of the place, a city where each and every soul depends upon the weight of words. I found a tiny rooming house of sorts. The tiniest of rooms, as it turned out, on Upper Hatch.

A garden flat with a sink in the room. The toilet was in a cramped little closet along the corridor. It was when I had opened the narrow window to the street that I spotted your mother. The sun had just wedged itself between two storm clouds and it poured down upon her. Her red hair like an apparition. And she turned. I was on the second floor, and she saw me. I nodded a hello from the upper floor, and she bowed in dramatic fashion, sweeping her outstretched arms as if she stood on stage, then quickly glared at me. I was taken aback, and shut the window. This sort of thing never used to annoy me, but that night, she was part of my troubling dreams. The next morning in search of tea, I spotted her walking ahead of me. A beautiful June morning. We both wound up at a take-away shop. She smiled coyly. The most heavenly face. She quickly apologized, and giggled a little. I didn't know what to say, but she filled the silence with a flood of words. Suddenly I was learning everything about her — her father a ship builder, her mother, a nanny, and she, a librarian at the National Library. We stood in the street, my own words punctuating hers, but mostly with questions. A steady stream, her lively green eyes as fresh as mint, her soft white hands drawing out one story after another. I loved her instantly. That night, we met at a pub, and pressed close to one another because it was so rowdy and noisy. Again, I listened, and was taken into a maze of tales and adventures. A soft rain was falling when we made our way down the street to her one-room flat. I was pretty exhausted — still jet-lagged from my trip from Canada — and when she set about to boil up some water for tea, I fell asleep. I woke six hours later, still fully clothed, but my shoes were at the foot of the bed, one neatly placed beside the other. She was gone, but had left a note that she was at the library. We would meet later. And we did. I checked out of the damp little rooming house room, and your mother and I began living together. It was cramped in her squared-off flat, but I had little in the way of things. Mostly just clothes, and a typewriter. A portable. I would set it up by the window in the mornings and work when she was away. I stayed with your mother for three months. We were married by the same priest who had baptized her 20 years before. I wore a suit that her father gave me, one that had been worn by his brother to family funerals. I loved your mother, maybe more than anyone.

The morning she told me she was pregnant, I did something inexcusable. I ran down the wooden steps to the street, and started walking. I wandered all over the city. I guess I thought I wanted her to have an abortion. She was Catholic. Her family wouldn't have allowed it. Besides, she wanted children. When I returned that night, she glared at me from the wooden chair by the window. My typewriter was packed away in its case, and sat next to the tattered leather suitcase on the floor. She didn't need to gesture to it. It was done. I told her that I loved her, but I didn't want a child. She looked away, her right arm slowly gesturing toward the door in the gloom of the flat. It was done. I picked up the bag, and the typewriter case.

Two nights later I was in London. I sent her a telegram to inform her of where I was staying. She never replied. I didn't hear from her until I was back in Canada — spring, the following year. A simple note, unsigned: *Your daughter Jessica is the eighth wonder of the world ... red hair like her mother.*

Dear Krysten

I was in Montreal when a friend of a friend of a friend offered me tickets for a Canadiens game. I came out of the Metro at the old Forum at the last moment. It was early October. Uncommonly warm night. The crowds were still circulating at Atwater and Ste. Catherine streets. I wended my way through the mingling throng, into the arena, and down to my seat. The puck had already been dropped. Next to me was a tall man who, within moments of me sliding into the seat beside him, had risen to his feet and left. He was frowning and silently pushed past the dark-haired woman next to him. That was your mother. She clearly was upset, fidgeting for some tissue. Glassy eyed. Her mind clearly not upon the game. Mind you, neither was mine. I was staring at her, and the empty arena seat yawned awkwardly between us. Finally, I spoke to her, and she pursed her lips, struggling to hold back a torrent of emotion. Then she spoke: *He's an ass*. I listened. This wasn't her husband. Not yet. He was her fiancé. A wedding planned for September. That wouldn't happen now, she said. Too much had gone down. He had had an affair seven months before, and she kept raising it with him, despite promises she'd never to mention it again. She had broken that promise countless times. Then she apologized for spewing this all out in such a rush to a stranger. I said nothing, but moved into the empty seat next to her, and clumsily put my left arm around her shoulders, and surprisingly, she leaned into me. She apologized. We were strangers. She continued. I listened. She certainly didn't need advice from someone married eight times. Your mother was such an elegant beauty — olive skin and winter dark eyes. When we left the game at the end of the second period, the Canadiens were ahead by two goals. I couldn't tell you who scored. I couldn't swear to anything about the game. We stepped out on to Ste. Catherine Street. It was the fall, and the air was warm. We waved down a taxi to take us to Le Spirite on Rue Ontario Est. Eclectic, crazy, cavernous, a décor of tin foil and mosaics, and that weird mixture of mellowy jazz. Your mother was hungry and polished off a huge bowl of leek soup, then a slab of chocolate cake. And I listened. By midnight, your mother was anxious to go home, and we parted. She really knew nothing about me — I had said so little. The next morning, I woke to her telephone call. She was working at a school on the west side of the city, and asked to meet me after work. We did. We met every night after work for about a month. She had ended her engagement. I finally wound up renting a small room in a boarding house. The room large enough to accommodate a sturdy arborite table, really a kitchen table, where I'd work in the mornings by the window light. Writing a novel. It was going well. Your mother and I spent our time going for walks, though occasionally we would while away the time at a café, or take in a film. Once or twice, we went to a hockey game. It was about a month into the relationship that she felt confident enough to come to my place. That night, we slept together, huddled on a single bed. We woke in the morning to the blinds suddenly springing to action, and rolling up unexpectedly. We jolted from the bed. I nearly fell to the floor. We laughed about it. Somehow we felt guilty. Your mother hurriedly dressed and rushed to work. She was still smiling when I saw her to the door. The landlady scowled at her as she went out. Three months later, we went down to city hall and made the arrangements. We were married in a civil marriage. The man presiding over it was a cousin to Jean Beliveau. We moved into a small flat above a tea shop, and life was good. I continued to work on the novel, and she at the elementary school. I'd wake up earlier and make porridge. Winter was upon us. I didn't own a winter coat, but your mother brought one home for me from her mother's. It had been her father's coat, and though it was big, it served the purpose. Montreal was cold. And I hated the cold. I longed for Barcelona, or maybe Marrakech. I begged her to quit her job. I calculated that we could move to Europe. I was making good money from stories I was writing. She kept refusing. I swear I didn't know she was pregnant with you when I left for Marrakech.

I found out at the Berber market when I went to find the man who would routinely signal to me to sit down and have a cup of mint tea. Every morning, I would stroll. I would watch him shift the large tin pot over the hot coals, and stuff fresh mint leaves into the steam. That morning, the boy who took care of my room and ran errands for me was suddenly standing beside me, out of breath. He told me of your birth. *Seven pounds. Dark eyes. The most beautiful angel. Your little girl. Please come back.* I drank the tea that morning, my insides burning. I made my way back to the rooms I rented by the month. It was near the old set that Hitchcock had used in 1956 for the opening scenes of *The Man Who Knew Too Much* with Doris Day and James Stewart. I smiled at the irony —I knew so little really. I felt compelled to send word back, and welcome you, but sadly I did not. I thought of your mother. I thought the others in my life, how I must seem to be such a cad. That morning I walked for two hours. Not sure where I went, or what I daydreamed. I was all over the map as my mind spun back to Bologna, Vienna and Prague. I should have written. So many times in my head, I composed letters but never put them to paper. I am now, and asking for this reunion. I see that you are playing hockey — I've read the notices in the paper. You grew up in Montreal, but now live in Windsor. From the photographs, you look so much like your mother. She was the sweetest. There are so many regrets. The biggest is leaving. I had wanted your mother to go away with me. I might not have left if I had known she was pregnant.

Tonight the nine of you drink red wine. The reunion of half-sisters is to say hello not goodbye. I tell each of you to catch the full moon that sails over the Seine, where the nine of you have gathered. We see the moon bobbing among the rooftops and spires. I swear it is smiling. That big self-satisfied grin on its face tells me it has an opinion. Should I care? Listen? Maybe it's time.

About the Author

Marty Gervais is a writer and photographer whose book *The Rumrunners* was a Canadian bestseller. He is the recipient of nearly 16 newspaper awards, the Queen's Jubilee Medal, and in 1998 won the prestigious Toronto's Harbourfront Festival Prize for his contributions to Canadian letters and to emerging writers. Gervais was Windsor's first poet laureate. In 1996, he was awarded the Milton Acorn People's Poetry Award for his book, Tearing Into A Summer Day. That book was awarded the City of Windsor Mayor's Award for literature. Gervais won this award again in 2003 for another collection, *To Be Now: New and Selected Poems*. His first published novel, *Reno*, appeared in 2005 from Mosaic Press, and was the runner-up in The International Three-Day Novel Writing contest. In 2006 Gervais and his work were the subject of a TV Bravo episode of the television series *Heart of A Poet* produced by Canadian filmmaker Maureen Judge.

CPSIA information can be obtained
at www.ICGtesting.com
Printed in the USA
LVHW091959250620
658993LV00009B/1835